ADAM AND THE CAPE

WRITTEN AND
ILLUSTRATED BY :
GINEKO VINCENT

There was a boy named Adam who had nothing to fear But every single thing scared him even the wind in his ear

SOMETIMES HIS
SHADOW WOULD GIVE
HE ONE CRAZY TYPE
OF FRIGHT
HE WOULD OFTEN BEG
HIS PARENTS TO STAY
IN THEIR BED AT NIGHT

ADAM WASN'T ALWAYS THIS WAY THERE WAS A REASON THIS WOULD BEGIN
ADAM DECIDED TO STAY UP LATE WAY PAST THE HOUR OF PAST THE HOUR OF 10

THIS WAS HIS PARENT'S MOVIE NIGHT ONE HE REALLY WANTED TO JOIN IT WAS ONE DAY A WEEK AND SINCE ADAM WASN'T INVITED, HE DECIDED TO SNEAK

WITH THEIR POPCORN POPPED COUCH
COMFY BLANKETS WARM AS TOAST
THE MOVIE CHOICE WAS MADE ADAM
SAW THE TITLE IT ENDED IN GHOST

AS ADAM WATCHED FROM BEHIND THE SOFA HE BECAME FROZEN WITH FEAR SOON ENOUGH HE WOULD LET OUT A LOUD SCREAM THAT MOMMY AND DADDY WOULD HEAR.

ADAM WHAT ARE YOU
DOING UP BUDDY? HIS
DAD WOULD ASK
BUT GETTING WORDS
FROM ADAM THAT
NIGHT WOULD NOT BE
A SIMPLE TASK

TIME WOULD PASS UNTIL AN IDEA WAS CLEAR
ADAMS PARENTS WOULD SHOW HIM SOME HERO MOVIES TO STOP THIS FEAR

THE FAMILY WATCHED THREE MOVIES THAT DAY IT WAS ALL SMILES THE FEAR WAS TAME
IT WAS THIS DAY ADAM NOTICED BRAVE HERO'S ALL HAD ONE THING THE SAME

IT WAS SIMPLE PLACED ON THEIR BACK
AND MADE THEM BRAVE WITH A
RECTANGLE SHAPE
ALL OF THESE HEROES HAD NO FEAR
BECAUSE OF THEIR CAPE

ADAM JUST KNEW IF HE COULD GET ONE OF
THESE AND PLACE UPON HIS BACK
THAT HE WOULD BECOME A HERO AND FEAR
COULD NEVER ATTACK

ADAM WOULD TELL HIS
PARENTS HIS PLAN AND
ASK NICELY IN THE
NICEST OF WAYS
AND TO ADAMS JOY
THERE SAT A BEAUTIFUL
RED CAP ON HIS BED IN
JUST A FEW DAYS

THIS CHANGED EVERYTHING
ADAM BEGAN TO BE BRAVER
THAN EVER BEFORE
BECAUSE HE HAD HIS RED
BRAVERY CAPE ON WITH
WHAT EVER HE WORE

ADAM HAD A NEIGHBOR A SWEET OLD LADY NAMED MRS. DUPREE
HE CAME TO HER RESCUE WHEN HER FAVORITE CAT MR. SNUGGLES GOT STUCK IN THE TREE

THE KID WITH THE BIKE WHO
WAS LEARNING TO RIDE
ONE DAY TOOK A TUMBLE
MAKING HER FALL TO DOWN
THE SIDE
SHE TRIED TO MOVE THE BIKE
ON HER OWN IT HAD FALLEN ON
HER ARM
JUST THEN RED CAPE ADAM
STEPPED IN TO HELP LIFT TO
STOP ALL HARM

ADAM FELT LIKE A TRUE HERO WITH BRAVERY
AND MIGHT
HE WAS NO LONGER AFRAID OF THE DARKNESS
BECAUSE HE SLEPT WITH HIS CAPE ON AT NIGHT

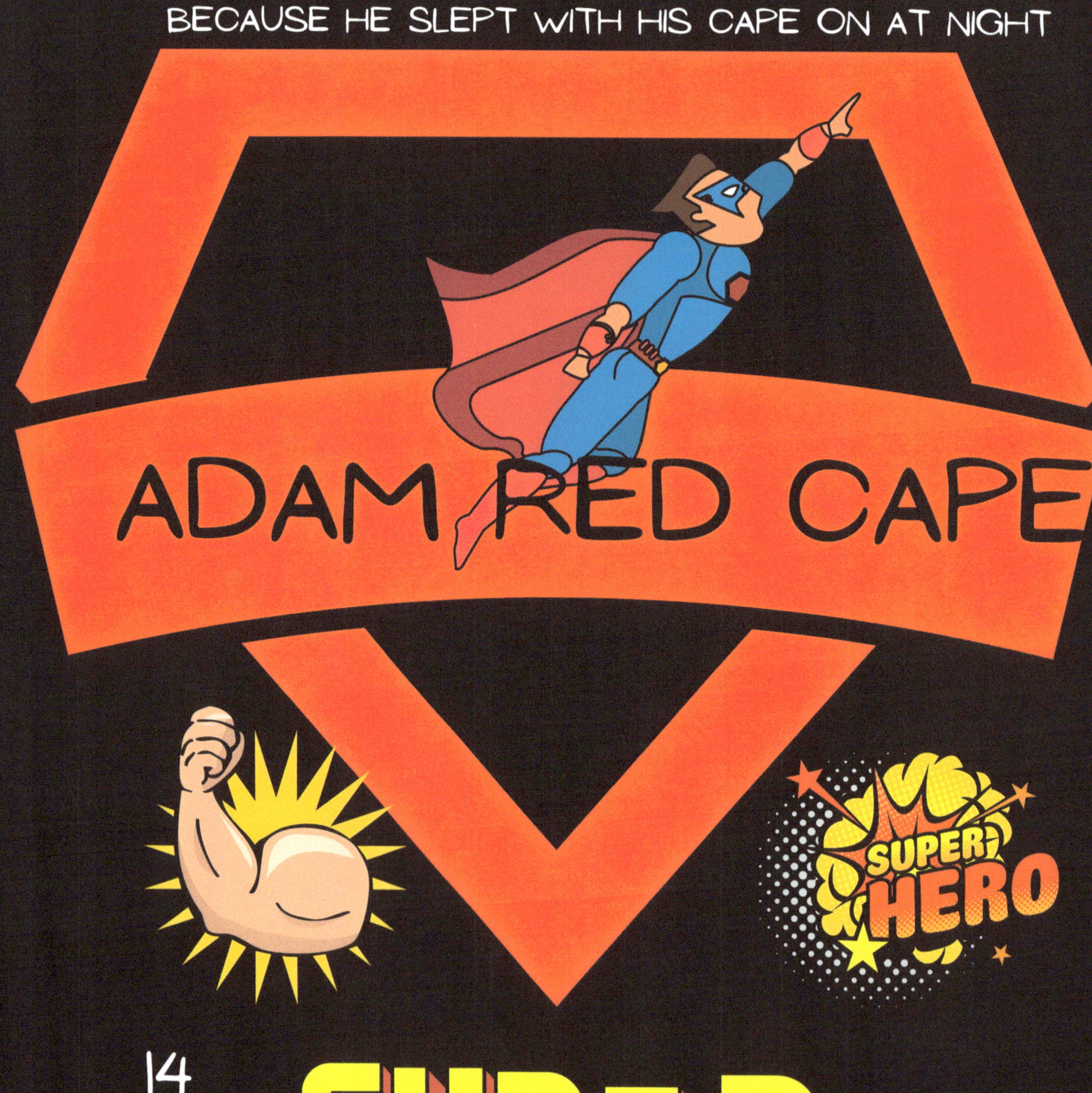

SUPE R

SOON A DAY WOULD COME WHEN ADAM WOULD
TRULY BE PUT TO THE TEST
BECAUSE THIS DAY MRS. DUPREE STARTED
COOKING AND DECIDED TO REST

THERE WAS SMOKE COMING FROM
HER KITCHEN WINDOW ADAMS
MOM WAS IN THE SHOWER
IT WAS ALL UP TO ADAM TO SAVE
HER HIM AND RED CAPE HAD THE
POWER

HE DIALED 911 TOLD THE PROBLEM AND ADDRESS IN A VERY CALM VOICE ADAM THEN CALLED MRS. DUPREE TO WAKE HER SHE MUST GO OUTSIDE SHE HAD NO CHOICE

ONE SECOND AFTER ADAM'S MOM CAME DOWN AND HE EXPLAINED ABOUT MRS. DUPREE SO THEY RUSHED OUTSIDE TO CHECK ON HER ADAM SAID THEY MUST GO SEE.

WHEN THEY ARRIVED THERE MRS. DUPREE WAS
UNHARMED SAFE AND SOUND
BUT SHE LOOKED PUZZLED AND CONCERNED
LOOKING AROUND AND AROUND
"MR. SNUGGLES" "MR. SNUGGLES" IN A SAD VOICE
SHE BEGAN TO CALL
ADAM JUST KNEW MR. SNUGGLES WAS IN THAT HOUSE AND NOT SAFE AT ALL

"MOM I'M GOING IN" HIS MOM SAID NO YOU'RE NOT WITH HIS CAPE IN HER HAND GRIPPED
BUT OFF TOOK ADAM MINUS THE CAPE THAT WITH A STRETCH HAD RIPPED

ADAM RAN IN AND CALLED FOR MR. SNUGGLES HE HAD NO FEAR AT ALL WITH SMOKE IN THE AIR
HE FOUND A LAZY MR. SNUGGLES RELAXING LICKING HIS FUR ON A CHAIR

ADAM RUSHED OVER TO GRAB HIM AND TAKE
HIM OUTSIDE WHERE THE AIR WAS PURE
SOON THE TWO WERE BACK TO SAFETY AND
NOW IN MIND HE WAS SURE

HE WAS A HERO THANKS TO RED CAPE HE
TOUCHED HIS BACK THAT DIDN'T GO AS PLANNED
THERE WAS NO CAPE THERE IT WAS GONE UNTIL
HE LOOKED UP THERE IT WAS IN HIS MOMS HAND

BUT HOW ADAM WONDERED HE KNEW HE HAD WENT IN ALONE AND HAD NO FEAR
HOW COULD HE HAVE BEEN SO BRAVE IF HIS RED CAPE WASN'T NEAR

ALL THIS TIME HE JUST KNEW THAT RED CAPE WAS GIVING HIM THE POWER TO BE TOUGH
HE ASKED HIS MOM HOW HE COULD HAVE DONE THIS HER REPLY WAS "ADAM YOU'VE ALWAYS BEEN ENOUGH"

IT WASN'T RED CAPE THAT GAVE HIM THE COURAGE IT'S SOMETHING HE'S ALWAYS HAD INSIDE
WHEN HE WORE RED CAPE IT WAS JUST ALONG FOR THE RIDE

ADAM WAS A BRAVE BOY
HE DIDN'T UNDERSTAND FROM THE START
BUT THIS DAY AND MOVING FORWARD HE UNDERSTOOD THAT HE NEED NOT FEAR BECAUSE HE HAD BRAVERY IN HIS HEART

NO CAPE NEEDED

THE END

www.ingramcontent.com/pod-product-compliance
Lightning Source LLC
LaVergne TN
LVHW071114160826
845679LV00004B/1072